GW00870598

Cinderella
at the ball

Ladybird

Cinderella lived in a castle with
her cruel stepmother
and stepsisters.

Life was hard, but Cinderella
was friends with the mice and
the birds.

One day the King sent out
invitations to a Grand Ball.
Cinderella was sad because she
had nothing to wear, except for
her mother's old dress.

But Cinderella's two favourite mice, Jaq and Gus, had an idea.

They found some pretty ribbon and some blue beads. The birds sewed them on and soon the old dress looked like new.

Cinderella loved the dress, but her stepsisters spoiled it.

Cinderella was very unhappy.
Then her fairy godmother
suddenly appeared with
a magic wand.

First she turned a pumpkin
into a coach. Then she
turned Cinderella's
friends the mice
into horses.

So Jaq and
Gus took
their friend
Cinderella
to the ball.
She was
wearing a
beautiful
new dress.

Jaq and Gus waited outside with the coach. Cinderella danced the night away with the Prince.

Cinderella was meant to leave at midnight but she left it too late. Jaq and Gus were mice again and the coach was no more. The friends ran home together.

Cinderella had left one glass slipper behind. The prince sent his footman out with it to search for his princess.

Cinderella's wicked stepmother locked her in her room.

But Jaq and Gus got the key and let her out– just in time.

So Cinderella and the prince
were married – and her friends
Jaq and Gus went to
the wedding.